The Chicken that could swim

written and illustrated by
Paul Adshead

Published by Child's Play (International) Ltd

© M. Twinn 1988   ISBN 0-85953-346-8 (limp)   Printed in Singapore
ISBN 0-85953-294-1 (cased)

In the garden, every day brings joy and sorrow.

For Rosemary, the snowy white duck,
this was a particularly joyful morning.
Rosemary had laid seven large, bluish-green eggs
and settled down to hatch them.

The Man who loves Birds was delighted.
On his calendar, he counted four weeks to the day
when the ducklings would hatch.

Rosemary's mate, Dorsington, was less confident.

"She can hardly sit still for four minutes,
let alone four weeks," he thought.

For Silky the chicken, it was a sad morning.
Silky wanted to hatch her eggs, too,
not provide them for the man's breakfast.
She was so unhappy that she couldn't lay
any eggs at all that day.

The man understood, but he thought:

"If she doesn't lay any eggs,
how can I let her hatch them?"

He began to wish he had not just eaten
the very last one that morning.

In the evening, there was even more bad news.
Rosemary was already bored stiff.
At first it had seemed fun,
but in less than an hour
she had begun to fidget.

By the time the sun set,
she felt hot, tired, hungry and thirsty.
She longed to dive into the cool, green water.

From her hiding place in the reeds,
she watched the other ducks
enjoying their evening swim.
It was more than she could take sitting down.

"Wait for me!" she quacked.

Then, with a tremendous splash,
she threw herself into the pond.
The eggs were soon forgotten.
They would go cold and never hatch.

Fortunately, the man came by just in time,
and he had a brainwave.

Moments later, he had put on his wellies
and was scrambling over the rocks and plants
beside the pond. One by one, he lifted
the seven duck eggs out of the nest,
and placed them carefully inside a basket.

Rosemary was far too busy to notice.
She was catching her supper.
(The black and wiggly kind that swims very fast).

He took the basket into the chicken cabin and
gently placed the sleepy Silky
on top of the eggs.

In the morning, she was so excited
and her mind so full of motherly thoughts,
that she did not even wonder
where the eggs had come from.

Silky drifted dozily through the next three weeks.
Her days passed in a contented trance
and her nights were filled with happy dreams.
Then, something inside her told her that the eggs
should have been fluffy yellow chicks by now.

But duck eggs take seven days longer to hatch.

Silky was instinctively wise.
She could sense movement within the eggs,
and was determined not to give up.

"Perhaps – tomorrow," she sighed to herself.

During the twenty-eighth night,
Silky finally heard the sound
she had been longing to hear.
A gentle tapping noise from within the eggs.
By dawn, the shells were beginning to crack open.

The Man who loves Birds woke up and checked his calendar.
It was the day he had been waiting for, too,
because the eggs needed to be returned
to their real mother before they hatched.

But now he had another problem.
How would Silky feel when
the eggs were taken away?

"One, two, three, four, five, six."

The man counted the eggs as he lifted them out,
but the seventh had almost completely hatched already.
He looked at the worried expression on Silky's face,
and decided to leave it for her.

Then he hurried down the garden with the others
and slipped them under Rosemary, who was still fast asleep.
Just in time. The cracks in the eggs were widening by the minute.

"Good, everything has worked out fine."

When Rosemary woke, her tummy felt bumbly and strange.

"It must have been those slugs
I ate for supper," she groaned.
"Perhaps if I stand up, I'll feel better."

But when she stood up, she felt stranger than ever.
In fact, she felt quite faint with shock.
For there in the nest were six newly hatched ducklings.

"Mother, MOTHER!" they all quacked.

(That's what *all* ducklings say to the first thing they see.)

Meanwhile, a bright orange beak
peeped from under Silky's soft white wing.
''MOTHER!'' it quacked.

The strange noise made Silky turn her head and stare.
Two anxious eyes peered up at her face.

''Yes, I'm your mother,'' clucked Silky tenderly.
''And your name is Nugget, because you are
the most golden chick I have ever seen.''

Silky was so proud, that she couldn't wait to show off
her new baby to the neighbours. But even she could not help
noticing certain unusual features in her pride and joy.

"Her feet are too big and flat,
and her beak is peculiar."

Before long, she met Voytek the cockerel and his mate Malenka.
Like all their Polish ancestors, they have long head feathers
which make them rather short-sighted. They peered at Nugget.

"What a beautiful little chicken," crowed Voytek.

"So like its mother," added Malenka.

"I'm hungry, Mother," quacked Nugget.

Silky began to scratch on the ground for food.
So did Aunt Malenka, Aunt Frizzle,
Uncle Voytek and Great Aunt Flippatina.

Nugget tried to do the same,
but her feet were quite the wrong shape
and the dust made her cough.

"May I have a drink, Mother?"

"There is a bowl of water over there," answered Silky,
pointing with her little grey beak.

"But do not go near the pond.
We chickens aren't meant to swim
and you would drown in a moment if you fell in."

Just in case, Silky followed Nugget
so that she could keep an eye on her.

When she saw the pond,
Nugget remembered Silky's words.
But she couldn't help herself.

Her feet headed past the bowl towards the pond
and she just couldn't stop them.

On the bank she paused. Then saw her reflection.
She gazed wide-eyed at her enormous orange beak.

"I don't look like Mother at all," she sighed.
She leaned over further and further
until she was balanced on the very tips
of her large webbed feet.

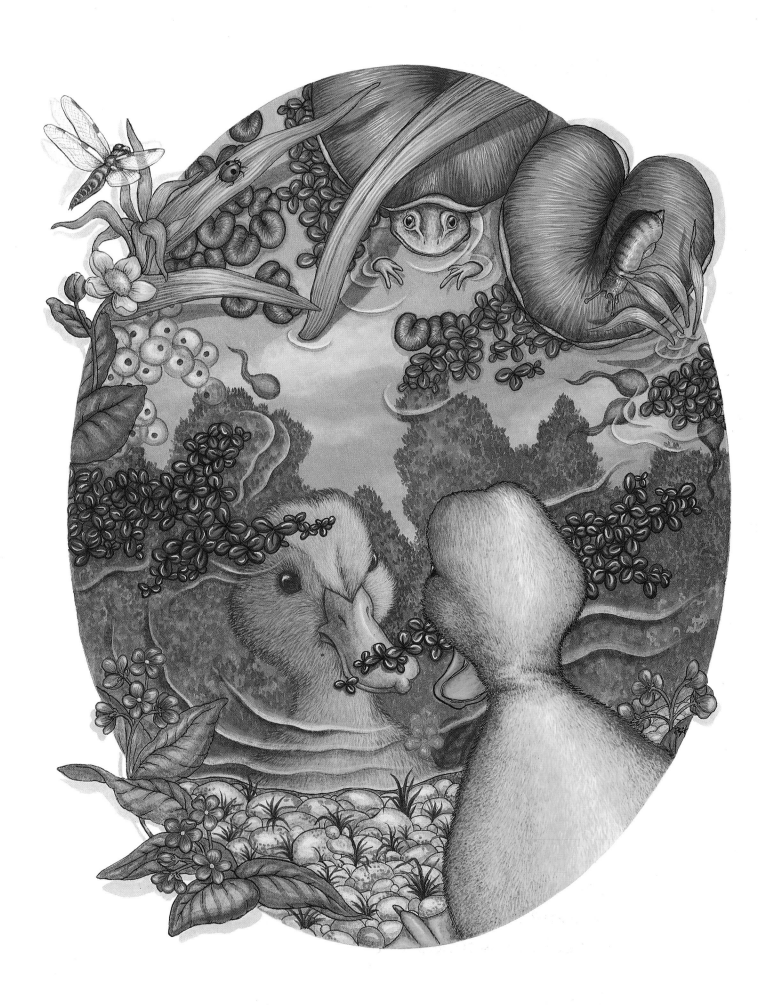

At that very moment, Rosemary woke up and saw Nugget.
Thinking that one of her own brood had left the nest,
she gave a very cross, very loud QUACK!

Nugget jumped, overbalanced, and,
before she could stop herself,
fell with an awful splash
and disappeared under the cold, green water.

Moments later she bobbed back to the surface, gasping for breath.

"Mother, Mother," she spluttered.
"Help me, I'm sinking!"

Silky rushed to the pond clucking with horror.
But Nugget wasn't sinking at all. She was floating beautifully,
and with each wave of her big paddle-shaped feet
she skimmed across the water like a speedboat.

Meanwhile, Rosemary had glided across the pond,
with her six little ducklings paddling furiously behind.

"Wait for us," they called breathlessly.

Soon they surrounded Nugget.
It was almost impossible to tell them apart.

"Why did you leave the nest
without your brothers and sisters?" scolded Rosemary.
"Come to your mother, at once."

"You're not my mother," said Nugget,
"and I don't have any brothers and sisters.
I'm an only chick."

The other ducklings laughed so much,
they bobbed up and down in the pond.

As she watched the ducklings swim away,
Nugget wanted to follow.
She thought about her reflection.
She felt very confused.

"Mother said that chickens can't swim.
But swimming is fun!
Am I a duckling after all?"

Silky was beside herself with worry.
She clucked and cackled so loudly,
that Toby the Yorkshire terrier, heard her
and barked to be let out.

The Man who loves Birds stood at the door and
stared after him as he rushed out of sight.
Every creature in the garden
seemed to be hurrying towards the pond.
The barking, clucking and quacking
grew louder and louder.

"What a commotion," he thought.
"Whatever can it be?"

He ran across the lawn
as fast as his old bones would carry him.

He was the last to arrive.

As he knelt by the pond,
something wonderful happened.
A damp little duckling waddled
out of the water and snuggled
under a fluffy white chicken.

"Mother," quacked Nugget.
"I'm not a duckling.
I am a swimming chicken."

So Nugget stayed with Silky.

As the weeks passed by,
she changed
from a tiny golden ball of fluff
into a beautiful snowy white duck.

During the day she was a duckling just like any other, splashing in the pond with her brothers and sisters.

But every evening she would waddle into the hen cabin to roost with her mother and the other chickens.

And that's the end of the story.
Almost but not quite . . .

This Spring, Nugget laid some eggs of her own
and settled down to hatch them.

"You'll never sit still for a full month,"
quacked Bertram, her mate.

But she did.

"You see," she explained,
"I'm not a duck, I'm a swimming chicken.
Come along children, it's time
you met your grandmother."